Summer Shadows

The **My Magical Pony** series:

Other series by Jenny Oldfield:

My Magical Pony

Summer Shadows

By Jenny Oldfield

Illustrated by Alasdair Bright

Hodder
Children's
Books

A division of Hodder Headline Limited

Chapter One

Krista stood in a sunny field full of
ponies. They trotted towards her, swishing
their tails.

"Hi, Comanche!" she grinned. "Hi, Misty.
Hi, Shandy."

Comanche came up and nuzzled her hand.

"Hey, I don't have any treats for you!"
She laughed as the friendly pony's soft, pink
nose searched in her pockets for an apple or a
piece of carrot.

In the far corner of the field, Drifter kept
his distance.

My Magical Pony

Krista fastened a head collar around Comanche's head and led him towards the gate. "You're a good boy," she told him. He was always pleased to see her, always ready to come into the stable yard and be saddled up.

Comanche plodded steadily behind Krista into the yard, where they found Jo Weston, the owner of Hartfell Stables.

"It's half past eight," Jo pointed out.
"We need to get a move on to be ready for
the first trek at nine."

So Krista left Comanche with Jo and ran
back to the field to fetch Misty. "Good girl,"
she told the grey, trotting her quickly out
of the field into the yard then dashing back
for Shandy.

"We're going to be busy," she said, parting
the dark bay pony's thick mane and buckling
the head collar. "Today's the first day of the
school summer holidays – yippee!"

Back in the yard Jo had already tacked up
Comanche and Misty.

"Shall I fetch Drifter?" Krista asked.

My Magical Pony

"Yes, quick as you can, please," Jo said, disappearing into the tack room to fetch a third saddle.

Krista ran back eagerly to the field. Drifter was a young chestnut pony who had only been at Hartfell for a few months. He was high-spirited and beautiful, with his glossy brown coat and white star between his gorgeous brown eyes. "Here, Drifter!" Krista called from the gate.

The pony tossed his head and began to gallop towards her. His long mane streamed back from his face, his hooves kicked up small chunks of earth.

"Whoa!" Krista said as he drew near.

Drifter stopped ten metres from where

she stood. He waited for her to walk to within arm's length, then suddenly ducked his head and trotted off.

"Come here, boy!" she called again.

He cocked his head to one side as if to say, *Come and get me!*

"OK," Krista told him, advancing steadily, head collar in hand. "Stand!" she said firmly.

Drifter tossed his head again. *No way!* And he was gone, cantering across the empty field, flicking his tail. He knew that Krista could only stand and watch as he took refuge from the sun in the shade of an old chestnut tree.

Krista shook her head. He was a lovely pony, but even she had to admit he could be a handful. *It's because he's so clever,* she reminded herself.

When he sees me with the head collar he knows he has to do some work. That's why he runs away!

"OK, if that's the way you want to play it!" she called, pretending to close the gate and

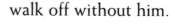

walk off without him.

Drifter watched with his head still to one side. *What's she up to?*

"Stay there by yourself if you want!" she called over her shoulder. "See if I care!"

Huh? She's leaving me in the field all by myself. I don't like this! Anxiously, the chestnut trotted to the gate.

"Hah, so you don't want to be left behind after all!" Krista grinned, quickly slipping the collar over the mischievous pony's head. "I know your game, you little monkey!"

Drifter nuzzled her arm as if to say sorry. And when they arrived in the yard he stood patiently as Jo saddled him and told Krista that she would be leading the ride on the little chestnut.

"Cool!" Krista ran for her hard hat and riding crop.

"Follow the cliff path around Whitton Bay," Jo instructed. "Mark will be riding Shandy and I've saddled Comanche for Carrie. Janey will be on Misty."

My Magical Pony

Krista nodded at the three young riders who had just been dropped off at the yard. She knew Mark Liddell and Carrie Jordan from school, but she'd never met the other girl before. "Hi, I'm Krista," she said.

"I'm Janey Bellwood. I'm new."

"Janey's ridden before," Jo explained. "So there shouldn't be any problems."

"I used to have a pony of my own," the girl said proudly.

Krista smiled and nodded. This was going to be fun!

"Ready, everyone?" Jo asked.

Mark, Carrie and Janey nodded.

"Let's go!" Krista called, heading Drifter out through the gate, up the lane, and along the narrow track that overlooked the spectacular golden bay.

"I led the ride!" Krista told Spike when she got home that evening. She was lying on her back staring up at the cloudless blue sky.

Spike the hedgehog drank milk from his saucer in the back garden of High Point Farm.

"I did – I led three riders!" Krista insisted. "I was on Drifter. It was cool!"

Slurp-slurp! Spike guzzled happily.

15

"OK, so it's nothing to you," she admitted. "But it was a big deal for me. We rode along the cliff path, past the magic spot …"

Slurp! Spike finished off the milk.

"… Where Shining Star usually appears," Krista confided. "He didn't show up this morning though, 'cos we don't need him right now."

She paused to let her pet hedgehog sniff around the rim of his empty saucer, wishing that she *had* seen Star, her magical pony.

In her mind's eye she pictured him appearing in his cloud of glittering mist, with his sparkling white coat that gave off a silver glow.

Rolling over on to her hands and knees,

she followed Spike across the lawn. "I can tell you about Shining Star," she giggled, "because you're the only one who can't give away the secret!"

Spike stopped, turned on the spot and began to dig with his sharp front paws.

"Krista, don't let Spike dig up my lawn!" her dad's voice interrupted.

Krista jumped. She sprang to her feet. "He's only looking for bugs and beetles!"

Her dad laughed. "Sorry, did I startle you?"

She nodded. How much had he heard?

"Did I hear you say there's a new pony called Star at Jo's stables?"

"Yes – no – yes!" Krista stammered. "Maybe. I don't know!" This was too close for comfort!

"Make up your mind," her dad laughed,
then luckily he changed the subject.
"Anyhow, Mum says to tell you tea's ready."

She took a deep breath and told him
she'd come in a few seconds. "Nearly!" she
whispered to Spike as her dad went back into
the house. She laughed and wagged her finger
at the puzzled little hedgehog. "Remember,
Spike, don't tell anyone about Shining Star.
He's magic and he's a secret. No one must
ever know!"

Chapter Two

"We're having a heatwave!" Jo looked up at the blue sky. She'd tethered the ponies in the shade to keep them cool.

It was the second day of the holidays. Krista slipped her foot into the stirrup and mounted Drifter. The chestnut pony skittered sideways as she adjusted the girth. "Whoa!" Krista ordered.

"How was he to catch this morning?" Jo asked as she helped other riders into the saddle.

"The same!" Krista grinned. Drifter had kicked up his heels and cantered off as usual.

And he was still in one of his silly moods, prancing about the yard, snorting and pulling at the reins.

"OK, Janey, up you go!" Helping the  newcomer on to Misty's back, Jo stood to one side.

"Whoa!" Krista told Drifter.

The pony shook his head then pranced towards Janey and her pony. Misty bared her teeth and stretched her neck, jerking the reins out of her rider's hands.

"Whoops, there you go!" Jo hurried forward to put things right. She frowned at Drifter and told him to behave. "I think Apollo and I had better lead the ride down to the beach this morning, since Drifter's in that daft frame of mind."

Krista nodded. "Sorry," she said to Janey, who smiled back.

Soon the group of six riders was ready to leave. They made their way down the lane, the ponies walking lazily because of the heat. When they reached the beach, Jo waited for the stragglers then told everyone they could gallop their ponies along the shore. She set off first on Apollo, while

Krista held Drifter back to bring up the rear.

"You go first," she said to Janey, who had held Misty back until second-to-last.

Janey kicked Misty's sides and off they went.

"OK," Krista told an impatient Drifter. "Now it's your turn!"

Relaxing the reins, they took off. The wind rushed against her, the cool sea spray foamed around the pony's feet. *Wow!* Krista thought.

Drifter's hooves thundered over the wet sand. The sea glittered. There wasn't a cloud in the sky.

"Watch out, Janey!" Krista warned as Drifter caught up with the grey pony. They were racing neck and neck.

Suddenly Krista imagined she saw something

in the white spray beside them. It was a ghostly shape, rising out of the foam, becoming a horse's head. Then its neck and shimmering white body seemed to appear. "Shining Star!" Krista gasped.

But Misty and Drifter galloped on and the dream shape vanished.

"This is cool!" an excited Janey cried at the far end of the bay. Her fair hair had escaped from under her black hat, her blue eyes sparkled.

"You're a good rider!" Krista told her.

"Thanks. So are you!"

Krista turned in the saddle to look back the way they'd come, half expecting still to see Shining Star galloping after them in the white foam. She searched hard, her heart pounding in her chest, willing her magical pony to appear. But there was nothing.

"Give your ponies a rest," Jo ordered.

After five minutes she asked who wanted another run along the beach.

"Me!" everyone cried.

And once more they set off at a gallop along the sands.

Chapter Three

It was weird how quickly time sped by during the school holiday, Krista thought. It was already Friday and she'd had a whole week of helping out at Hartfell. Every morning she'd brought in the ponies, twice a day she'd groomed them and cleaned the tack before taking each pony back out into the field.

"We never see anything of you!" her mum had complained early that morning, before Krista had ridden off on her bike. "Why can't you have a day off from the stables and take a proper holiday?"

"Yes, and pigs might fly!" her dad had laughed.

Both her mum and dad knew that ponies meant more than anything in the world to Krista.

Anyway, Jo was always glad of her help. "Hi Krista, you're bright and early as usual!" the stable owner called as she cycled into the yard. "How do you fancy riding somebody different today?"

"Not Drifter?" Krista checked. She'd had a great week riding the lively pony, even though catching him each morning had been hard.

"No. I thought maybe young Janey Bellwood could ride him out. She's a decent little horsewoman. I'm sure she can handle Drifter."

"Cool!" Krista nodded. "I'll ride Misty instead."

And so it was decided, and when Janey arrived with her mum Krista ran to tell her the news.

The words were hardly out of Krista's mouth before Janey rammed her hat on her head and sprinted towards the chestnut pony.

"Are you sure this is a good idea?" a nervous Mrs Bellwood asked. She was a small, timid woman who looked like she didn't spend much time around horses. "That brown one always seems too lively for my liking."

"Janey will be fine," Krista assured her.

My Magical Pony

"And Drifter isn't half as bad as he looks, especially for Janey. She's a great rider!"

Once more she'd hardly finished the sentence before there was a loud neigh and a clattering of hooves.

"Watch out!" Jo yelled.

Krista spun round in time to see Janey on Drifter, her legs out of the stirrups, the reins loose, charging across the yard towards her and Mrs Bellwood.

"Hang on, Janey!" Krista called, standing with her feet apart and her arms flung wide to make the runaway pony swerve to the left, up against the tack room wall.

Janey held tight, lurching forward as Drifter came to his sudden halt.

"What happened?" Krista cried, helping Janey down to the ground.

"I don't know. He just reared up the second I sat in the saddle. Then he raced off."

Jo came running, her face fixed in a deep frown. "Are you OK?" she checked with Janey.

Mrs Bellwood stepped in before her daughter could answer. "No, of course she's not all right! She almost had a terrible accident because of that stupid pony!"

"Mum!" Janey protested. "I'm OK, honestly!"

Krista took hold of Drifter's reins and calmed him down.

"Krista, take Drifter into his stable,"

Summer Shadows

Jo said, as Janey's mother launched into a long complaint.

"Even I can see that the creature isn't properly trained, and I know nothing about horses! How could you think of putting poor Janey on his back?"

"Come on, boy!" Krista murmured. The sooner he was safe in his stable the better.

As she led him away she heard Jo say sorry and Janey plead with her mum not to make a fuss.

A few minutes later, Jo came to talk to Krista in the stable. "Drifter won't be coming on the trek this morning," she said. "I've put Janey back on Misty."

Krista nodded. "Shall I take his saddle off and work him in the paddock instead?"

Jo shrugged. "You can if you like, but to be honest I've had enough of this little chestnut for one day!"

In the corner of his stable, knowing he was in disgrace, Drifter hung his head.

"I'll lunge him," Krista decided. That way she would get rid of some of his pent-up energy.

Shaking her head and sighing, the usually cheerful Jo said Krista could do as she pleased.

"Oh, Drifter!" Krista said, tutting and quietly loosening his girth. "Everyone thinks you've been naughty. Now we'll have to

go out there into that paddock and show
how good you can be!"

Out in the paddock on the end of a long
lunge rein, Drifter was good as gold.
He walked when Krista asked him, then

trotted and cantered in neat, balanced circles.

"Good boy!" Krista told him, slowing him to a walk once more. She loved his smooth changes of pace and the way the sun made his coat gleam bright chestnut. "And now I know why you reared up!" she murmured, drawing in the long rein until the pony was close enough to stroke.

Drifter nuzzled her shoulder.

"I'll tell Jo when she gets back from the ride," Krista promised, remembering the sharp thistle she'd found under Drifter's saddle when she'd lifted it off his back and returned it to the tack room. The thistle had been stuck to the pony's saddle blanket – a sharp ball of tiny thorns that would have pricked his skin the moment Janey had sat down. "I bet it hurt!" she whispered, softly stroking the bright white star between his eyes.

Drifter gave a low whinny. He pricked his ears and seemed to pay attention to something which Krista couldn't make out.

"What is it?" she murmured, glancing up. There was only a gentle breeze which lifted the hair on the pony's fetlock, and perhaps a light white cloud in the sky that hadn't been there a moment before. *Shining Star!* Krista thought, feeling goose-pimples on her bare arms. She looked and listened – nothing!

Drifter stamped his front hoof and nudged her arm.

"OK, let's do some more work," she said, putting thoughts about her magical pony to one side.

She sent Drifter out to the end of the lunge rein and set him trotting again, hardly noticing when Jo returned with her riders. "Good boy!" she told him over and over, watching him pick up his feet perfectly and carry his neck beautifully, neck arched, ears pricked.

"Krista!" Jo called after a while.

Krista and Drifter had been working so hard that they hadn't noticed Jo at the paddock gate. Krista reined the pony in and led him across. "He's been so good!" she began.

Jo stopped her. "Listen to me, Krista. I've made a decision."

Krista frowned. Suddenly she felt as if she'd upset Jo, that there was a bad feeling in the air. "What kind of decision?"

"About Drifter. It's not been an easy one to make, but I've been thinking about it all the time I was out on the ride."

As Jo hesitated Krista felt more and more uneasy. "He's just worked really hard," she protested.

"He almost threw Janey off," Jo cut in.

"Yes, but—"

"Stop!" Jo held up her hand. "Nothing you say will make me change my mind. Drifter is a young pony, but he's been here six months and I've given him every chance to settle down. Yet still I can't trust him with most riders we get here at Hartfell."

"This morning wasn't Drifter's fault!" Krista cried. "I'm sure Janey could ride him if we tried again."

But Jo shook her head. "Mrs Bellwood wouldn't allow it," she pointed out. "No, Krista – Drifter is never going to be a good riding-school pony. For a start, he's almost impossible to catch."

Krista swallowed hard. She dreaded what was coming next.

"Then when we do manage to bring him in from the field, he prances and dances around the yard, setting the others on edge. On top of that, he's too high-spirited out on the trail."

At Krista's side the chestnut pony lowered his head. She put an arm around his neck.

"It's no good hoping that I'll change my mind," Jo warned.

"What are you planning to do?" Krista whispered.

"It's sad, but Drifter can't stay here," Jo told her steadily. "I've decided to send him back to where he came from."

"To Berryfields!" Krista gasped.

Jo nodded and turned quickly away. "I just rang Melanie Bird. She's willing to take him back."

"But you can't!" Krista begged, standing helplessly with Drifter by the paddock gate. It was the worst thing that could possibly happen!

"I can and I will," Jo told her, walking swiftly on. "Melanie says she'll send a trailer to collect him first thing in the morning."

Chapter Four

Drifter knew that something was wrong as Krista unsaddled him in the yard and led him towards his field. He walked quietly past Mark, Janey and a small group of riders.

"Come on, boy!" Krista's quiet words were choked by the tears she was trying not to shed.

"What's wrong with her?" Mark asked.

"I've decided to send Drifter away," Jo explained. "So Krista's a bit upset."

A bit upset! As Krista reached Drifter's empty field, she let the tears fall. "Go on, off you go, boy!" she told the puzzled pony.

He hung his head and nuzzled her arm, as if asking why she was crying and how come he wasn't needed for the afternoon ride.

Krista stroked his nose and rubbed his bony forehead. "Go!" she said again. His warm breath and sweet smell were too much to bear.

She watched as he trotted nervously across the grass then broke into a gallop around the field.

"Hey, Krista!" a quiet voice said.

She turned to see Janey standing by the gate. Quickly wiping her wet cheeks with the back of her hand, she went to join her.

"I hear Drifter's leaving," Janey said sadly.

"He's going back to Berryfields."

"Is that bad?"

Krista nodded. "Very bad. Berryfields is run by a woman called Melanie Bird. She buys and sells horses."

Janey listened thoughtfully. "So Drifter won't stay there long? He'll get a new owner."

"Maybe," Krista frowned. "The trouble is, Melanie will have to tell people why Drifter was sent away from Hartfell."

"So everyone will think he's hard to ride and nobody will want him?"

"Or else he'll get sold to a bad owner," Krista said. "It's not fair for poor Drifter, especially now that I know why he bolted across the yard with you this morning."

"You do?" Janey watched the lonely pony finish his gallop and come trotting back towards them.

"Yes. I found a thistle under his saddle pad," Krista explained. "It must have made him jump."

Janey shook her head. "I wish I'd been able to hold him back instead of letting him bolt."

"It's not your fault," Krista said quickly. "But it's not Drifter's either."

The two girls stood in silence for a while, watching the beautiful chestnut trot alongside the hedge then break into another gallop. He stopped in the shade spread by the wide branches of the chestnut tree.

"It's so sad!" Janey sighed.

"Totally," Krista agreed. *Poor Drifter.*
Tomorrow he would leave in a trailer for
an unknown future. She would never see
him again.

"What's up, love?" Krista's mum asked after
she got home later that evening. "Why are
you moping around the house?"

"No reason," Krista fibbed. All afternoon she'd kept busy at the stables, trying not to think about Drifter. She'd cleaned tack and swept the yard. Then she'd fed Lucy and Holly, Jo's two black cats. Afterwards, she'd groomed Scottie, the ex-racehorse, and picked out his hooves. But when she'd finished her work and had set off for home on her bike, she'd stopped to peer over the hedge into Drifter's field.

"You're not yourself," her mum insisted, putting an arm around her shoulder. "Come on, spill the beans!"

Krista had looked over the hedge and Drifter had been close by. He'd trotted up to her, whinnying with pleasure. She'd seen the eager look in his dark brown eyes and the spring in his step, and it had broken her heart.

"Jo is getting rid of Drifter because he's too much of a handful," she told her mum. "He has to leave Hartfell!"

Chapter Five

That night Krista lay awake for hours, staring out of the window. She watched the summer sky turn pink then darken, she saw a thin crescent moon rise.

"Shining Star, I need you!" she said over and over, praying that her magical pony would appear.

When she fell asleep she dreamed of a pony flying through the dark sky, beating his powerful white wings. He scattered silver dust in his flight between the stars, he soared over the moorland hills, sweeping down towards the glittering bay.

But when she woke up it was a bright Saturday morning, and there was no sign of Shining Star.

I'll cycle along the cliff path, Krista decided. *Maybe Star will be there!*

"You don't have to go to the stables today if you don't want to," her mum had said over breakfast. "It might be too hard for you to watch Drifter being loaded into the trailer and taken away."

But Krista had decided to be there. "I have to say goodbye," she'd insisted. And she'd set off as usual.

Now, as she cycled the narrow path,

glancing down at
Whitton Bay and up at
the rocky horizon, Krista's
heart beat faster.

Please come! she pleaded
silently to Shining Star.
Help me save Drifter before it's too late!
She stopped on the magic spot.
Down below, the waves broke on to the
sandy shore. Above her head, a white seagull
floated on an air current then suddenly
swooped down to the sea.

It was no good. Star must be busy helping
someone else with his magic powers. Slowly
she cycled on towards Hartfell.

*

Summer Shadows

Krista arrived at the stable to find a Land Rover and trailer parked in the yard. The red trailer had the name "Berryfields" painted in gold on the side. A ramp had been lowered. The inside of the trailer was lined with straw.

Krista's heart thumped against her ribs. Now she had to face the truth – Drifter was really leaving!

Quickly she went to the field where the ponies were kept, in time to see Jo leading Misty to the gate. Behind them stood Drifter, a lonely figure in the otherwise empty field.

"Drifter's up to his usual game," Jo told a man who held open the gate for her and the little grey. When she spotted Krista, she handed Misty over and with a spare head collar went back to fetch the chestnut.

"He's a handsome pony," the Berryfields driver commented drily. "It's a pity he doesn't have a good temperament to go along with his looks."

Krista frowned and led Misty into the yard.

"Hi Krista!" Janey called, leaning out of her car window.

Krista tethered Misty then went to join her. "You're early," she said.

Janey nodded then got out of the car. "I wanted to say bye to Drifter."

"Me too." But now that the moment had come, Krista almost wanted to change her mind and not be anywhere near. She heard the sound of hooves clip-clopping into the yard and turned to look.

Jo led Drifter towards the trailer. The pony saw it and stopped. Jo pulled the lead rope, urging him up the ramp.

"Get on there!" the driver grunted, giving the pony a sharp tap on the rump.

Startled, Drifter tugged away even harder. Jo had to use her full weight to stop him.

"I hate this!" Janey whispered.

Again the man slapped the pony and made him pull away in panic.

"No need for that!" Jo spoke sharply. She stepped on to the ramp herself then offered Drifter a carrot from her pocket.

The trembling pony edged towards the carrot.

My Magical Pony

"Gently does it!" Jo breathed. Bit by bit she got him into the trailer.

Slam! The driver darted forward to raise the ramp and bolt it shut. Inside the trailer, Drifter whinnied and kicked out in fear against the metal sides. Jo emerged rapidly from the side door.

"This is awful!" Krista whispered to herself. Ponies hated being hemmed in and having doors slammed on them. She put her hands to her ears to block out the sounds.

The driver quickly shook hands with Jo. "I see now why you wanted rid of him," he muttered, quickly climbing into the Land Rover. Before anyone could speak, he had started the engine and begun to tow the trailer out of the yard.

In silence Janey, Jo and Krista watched him leave.

Krista caught a brief glimpse of Drifter's head turning towards them, his ears flat against his head, nostrils flared. "He's so scared!" she whispered.

There was another uncomfortable silence as the trailer rocked and rattled into the lane.

"Goodbye, Drifter!" Janey called.

Jo frowned and glanced at Krista. "I'm sorry I had to do this."

Krista nodded. There was a big lump in her throat as the trailer vanished from sight.

Chapter Six

After Drifter left the yard, the fun went out of Krista's summer, as if the sun had disappeared behind a big black cloud.

And yet, on the outside nothing was different. The days were still long and bright, Spike ambled around the garden at High Point, the ponies of Hartfell trekked out along the trails.

A week passed and the ponies ate down the lush green grass in the fields. In the second week, Jo drove the twenty miles to Berryfields and bought a new three-year-old pony to replace Drifter. She brought the light bay mare into the yard at Hartfell and carefully unloaded her.

Krista watched from across the yard.

"Isn't she sweet!" Carrie Jordan cried, rushing to greet the new arrival.

The little mare walked down the ramp of Jo's horse-box and took a cautious look at her new home. She was a milky coffee colour with almost black mane and tail.

"Look, she's nuzzling my hand!" Carrie announced. "She's so-oo pretty!"

Krista had to admit that the new pony was great in every way. First, she was a beautiful colour, second she was in fantastic condition, with her gleaming coat and silky mane –

not too fat and not too skinny. Third, she seemed laid back and at ease in her new surroundings. Still, Krista didn't rush to make a fuss of her as once she would have done.

"What's up with you?" Mark asked. He'd come out of the tack room and noticed Krista hanging around in the doorway.

"Nothing." She shook her head.

"Her name's Kiki," Jo told Carrie and Janey, who had just arrived. "We'll put her in a stable until the vet's taken a look at her and checked her over." Noticing Krista, she waved her across.

"What do you think?" Jo asked.

"She's lovely," Krista said, unable to stop the next question from popping out of her mouth. "Did you see Drifter at Berryfields?"

Jo nodded briskly. "Yes, he's still there. Melanie has put an ad about him in the local paper."

Krista sighed. *It's like we said — nobody wants to buy him!* "How was he?" she asked.

"He seemed OK," came the vague reply. Then Jo got busy with Kiki and the arrival of John Carter, the vet.

For sale – 3-year-old chestnut gelding. 13hh. Not a novice ride. Tel. Berryfields 607845.

Krista read the brief advert in the paper and knew it must be for Drifter. She read it five or six times with a sinking heart. She felt sure that the only person who would buy this kind of pony would be a bad owner – perhaps another dealer who would buy him cheap or someone with cruel ideas about how to "break" a horse's spirit. But what could she do?

"Have you seen this?" she asked Janey after a lesson in the paddock with Misty. "It's an advert for Drifter."

Summer Shadows

Janey read the ad quietly. "Maybe someone nice will buy him," she murmured.

She was called away by her mum, who beeped her horn impatiently.

"Or someone nasty!" Krista sighed.

Three weeks passed and news came to Hartfell that Drifter had at last been sold.

"Thank heavens!" Janey said to Krista when they heard that the chestnut pony had a new home.

"Yeah, maybe everything's OK!" Krista tried to believe that there would be a happy ending, but deep down she was still worried. "Do you know who bought him?" she asked Jo.

"A woman from Oxtoby, which is a village about five miles inland from here. That's all I know."

Oxtoby. Krista remembered the name. That evening she found her dad's local map and looked it up. The village was a little dot, with a cross for a church and only four or five houses.

"This is it!" she told Spike, spreading the map flat on the grass and letting him scuttle across it. She pointed with her finger. "This is Drifter's new home!"

The hedgehog snuffled and sniffed. There was nothing to eat, so he ambled steadily on.

Krista studied the map. "Five miles is not that far!" she muttered to herself.

Summer Shadows

*

I'm sure I could cycle there! she thought, wide
awake at midnight. *And I want to see him, to find
out how he is and to let him know I haven't forgotten
about him.* The more Krista thought about it,
the more sure she grew that it was the right
thing to do.

*If Shining Star was here, I could climb on his back
and fly!* she told herself. Once more, she
longed for her magical pony in vain.

It was a Saturday morning, two days after she'd
looked at the map, when Krista finally put her
plan into action.

Waving goodbye to her mum and dad,
she set off on her bike as if she was going

My Magical Pony

to Hartfell as usual, but soon turned off
the lane and whizzed down the hill into
Whitton. She cycled along the sea front,
past the pink, white and yellow hotels to a
crossroads, where a sign pointed her inland
towards Oxtoby.

Summer Shadows

For a while she cycled easily along a quiet, flat road, but then it grew hilly and hard. Soon Krista's legs began to ache.

What if I can't find Drifter when I get to the village? she wondered. *What if this is all a waste of time?* She knew too that Jo would soon be wondering where she was. *Maybe I should forget this,* she thought, cycling on downhill, almost ready to turn around and go back.

But at the bottom of the hill she came to a sign that said Oxtoby, and then a house, and beyond that the church she'd seen marked on the map. Krista put on her brakes and stopped.

What now? She looked around. It was true it was a tiny village, but still she couldn't tell which was Drifter's new home and she could hardly knock on people's doors to ask. So she wheeled her bike along the road until she reached the church gate.

I'll dump the bike, she thought, *and investigate some of these narrow footpaths.* Soon she was beating her way along overgrown paths, disturbing insects as she pushed aside the flowering bushes. For a while it seemed as if the quiet paths led nowhere, and certainly not to any fields that had ponies in them.

But then Krista came across an old wooden gate tied with frayed string. It led into a small field overgrown with buttercups and yellow ragwort, with no water and a broken-down shed in one corner – definitely not a field where anyone should keep a horse.

Krista heard a noise and climbed the gate for a better view. What she saw made her gasp in horror.

There was a pony in the field, but at first she did not recognise him. His brown coat was dull and dusty, his mane tangled, his hooves caked with dried mud. A closer look showed Krista that there were dirty wounds on his front legs that had scabbed over without being cleaned and that the pony was badly lame.

The chestnut raised his head at the sight of Krista. He looked dully in her direction.

"Drifter!" she cried, scarcely believing what she saw. Could this be the beautiful, lively, high-stepping Drifter she used to know? Only the white star on his forehead told her that

she was right. "What happened to you?"

He began to walk towards her, stumbling as he came across the rough ground. His head was hanging, his eyes dull.

But before he reached the gate, a woman came out of the tumbledown shed and started to yell.

"No trespassers!" she shouted, waving her arms at Krista and telling her to get off the gate.

Krista leapt to the ground.

The angry woman caught up with poor Drifter and pushed him away. "This is private property!" she warned. "I don't want kids trespassing on my land."

Backing off down the path, Krista saw that the middle-aged woman had a lined face and short brown hair. She was dressed in a green polo shirt and jeans, carrying a coiled rope and a bucket half full of dirty water.

"The path is private as well!" Drifter's new owner warned.

"I only wanted ..." Krista began.

My Magical Pony

"I don't care what you wanted!" The
woman jumped down Krista's throat before
she could finish her sentence. "All I'm
interested in is you leaving my property!"

"B-but …!" How could Krista leave Drifter
here, in these conditions?

Still the mean woman shooed her away.
"Go!" she ordered, putting down the bucket
and climbing over the gate. She stood with
her hands on her hips, glaring at Krista,
giving her no choice. "I'm warning you, if
you don't get out of here I'll call the police!"

Chapter Seven

There was nothing for it, Krista decided – she had to go to the magic spot.

"There's ragwort in that field!" she muttered aloud as she cycled as fast as she could. She knew that the weed was poisonous for horses. "If Drifter eats much of that, he could die!"

The quickest way was back into Whitton and up a flight of rough steps leading from the beach to the cliff path. Krista pedalled hard. She left her bike in the small car park overlooking the beach then sprinted across the sand.

My Magical Pony

Holidaymakers lolling in deckchairs
watched her run between the sandcastles then
went back to their newspapers and ice creams.

Once she reached the wooden steps,
Krista paused for breath. She looked up at
the steep cliff then began the hard climb.
Twenty steps, then forty and finally fifty as
she reached the top, where she glanced down
at the way she'd come. Now the people in
deckchairs looked like small specks in the
wide bay.

With weary legs and aching lungs, Krista
ran along the high path to the spot where
Shining Star had first appeared.

She stood in the lonely place, her head
tilted back, gazing up into the bright blue sky.

Summer Shadows

"Please come!"
she begged.
"Drifter needs our
help!"

Krista stared at
the endless sky.
Waiting was awful.
"Please, Shining
Star! He has no
water. His knees

are covered in scabs, and the worst thing
is the ragwort! I know he'll die if we don't
help him!"

She felt a breeze against her face. It raised
her hopes, but then faded.

"Why won't you come?" she cried, glancing

down at the shore and across at the wide horizon. She longed to see clouds and the mysterious shape of her magical pony flying through the calm air, but there was only a distant ship and the sea sparkling like diamonds.

Krista sat down on the grass beside the sandy track. Her hopes were dashed and she suddenly felt very tired. Covering her face with her hands, she tried not to cry.

"Krista?" a voice whispered.

She jumped up and spun around on the spot. She took in the sea and the dark headland of Black Point, then the dizzy sweep of dark moorland rising to the jagged horizon. And there, appearing over the brow of the hill was a faint wisp of cloud, growing bigger, billowing down the hill towards her.

"At last!" she breathed.

"Tell me about the danger you have found!" the mysterious voice said. "I am listening."

"It's to do with Drifter!" Krista explained, watching the cloud begin to shimmer and surround her with silver dust. "He's gone to a cruel owner who doesn't give him water or look after his wounds. She's put him in a field where there are poisonous weeds!"

Slowly the silver dust settled. A pair of dark eyes gazed at Krista, and then a head appeared, and a flowing white mane. Powerful wings beat in the air above Krista's head. "Yes, we must help him," Shining Star agreed.

Summer Shadows

The magical pony hovered above the path, giving off a soft silver light that made the mist glitter. He was beautiful as ever, with his pure white coat and arched neck, his front legs drawn up under him, his back legs trailing, ready to alight.

Now that Star was here, Krista smiled with relief.

"Climb up," he told her, his wings spread wide and beating gently. "Tell me where we must go."

"It's not far!" she promised, scrambling on to the pony's broad back. "But we have to hurry!"

Shining Star nodded and beat his wings more strongly. There was a rush of air and they were off the ground, hovering for a moment while Krista took hold of the pony's mane. "Which way?" Star asked.

She pointed inland, towards Oxtoby. Thank heavens Star was here at last! "We're coming, Drifter!" she called out. "Don't worry, everything is going to be all right!"

Shining Star flew swiftly over the moors with Krista on his back.

I know how it feels to be a bird! she thought, looking down on the farmhouse roofs and at the narrow ribbons of road winding their way across country. She loved the freedom of soaring through the air.

Then they came to the village of Oxtoby

and Krista held her breath as the magical
pony flew low over the church. "Almost
there!" she whispered, grasping Star's mane
with both hands and asking him to fly slowly
over the fields beyond the church.

Tilting his wings, he flew in a slow circle
until the telltale sign of the yellow ragwort
showed her the field where Drifter was kept.

"Here!" she cried, waiting until she felt
Shining Star's feet touch the ground before
she slid off his back.

The magical pony and Krista gazed around
the rough field that had become the little
chestnut's poisonous home.

"That's strange!" she murmured. "He's
not here."

"Perhaps he's inside the wooden building?"
Star suggested, trotting towards the old shed
in the corner of the field.

Krista ran with him. When they reached
the shed, she eased open the creaking door
and peered inside. "Puh!" The musty, animal
smell made her put her hand to her nose.
She made out piles of stale dung, wet straw
and dirty plastic sacks, but no Drifter. "He
was here!" she insisted.

"But not any more," Shining Star said.

Krista ran to search the edges of the
field and finally came back to the gate. She
noticed that the frayed twine holding it shut
on her first visit was now missing. "It's open!"
she said.

Summer Shadows

"Your pony has escaped from his cruel owner," Star guessed.

"Hmmm." Krista had dropped to her knees to examine the ground. She found deep hoof-prints and lots of scuffed soil, and then a metal shoe that had been kicked loose and fallen off. "I think there's been a struggle," she told Star, growing more certain as she  spotted long strands of chestnut horse hair caught in the bars of the gate and, worst of all, traces of blood on the white gate-post.

She stood up with a deep frown creasing her forehead. "This must have happened in the last hour," she told Shining Star.

"Drifter was definitely still here when I left to come and find you." Gingerly she reached out and touched the still-wet blood stains with her fingertips.

Star listened carefully. "Then the owner has taken him away," he said.

Krista nodded. "The woman was carrying a rope. Maybe she led him into another field!"

"Climb on!" the magical pony instructed. "We'll make a search."

No sooner said than Krista was on his back and they were flying once more – over the empty lanes and silent houses, past the old stone church.

"It's so quiet!" she muttered, still horrified by her discovery of the struggle by the gate.

Summer Shadows

What if poor Drifter had gashed himself or opened up the wounds on his knees and was bleeding badly?

Shining Star hovered over the churchyard, looking down on the rows of gravestones. Hearing the sound of a lawn mower from the patch of grass by the church gate, he decided to land.

"Ask the man with the machine," he told Krista. "I will stay here, out of sight."

So she ran as he told her, round the front of the church and found an old man with white hair and a moustache busily mowing. Krista startled him by running up to him and touching his arm.

"Oh my goodness!" he exclaimed, letting the motor die. "You gave me quite a fright!"

"I'm sorry, I didn't mean to! But have you by any chance seen a chestnut pony? He's missing from his field."

"A chestnut pony?" The man took out his hankie and mopped his brow. "Let me see now."

"He was in the field along the narrow path. It belongs to a lady with short hair, dressed in a green polo shirt …"

"Short hair … green polo shirt?"

Krista clenched her hands, hoping that the old man would be able to help. Otherwise she and Shining Star would have to begin their search all over again.

"Ah yes!" he said, noisily blowing his nose before he put his hankie back in his pocket. "You must mean Susan Owen at Lane End!"

Krista nodded. "Does she have a chestnut pony that she bought from Berryfields?"

"I believe she does. In fact, I hear that she bought the pony for her daughter, though neither of them knows anything about horses. They came from the city, you know – not country folk at all."

"And have you seen her lately?" Krista asked eagerly. Now she understood why Drifter had been so badly treated. It must be because the Owens didn't know even the basic rules about taking care of a pony.

The old man nodded. "As a matter of fact, I have."

"And?" she prompted.

"She brought the poor creature down her path by the side of the churchyard here. It was about half an hour ago. I was busy so I didn't pay much attention. But I did notice the pony was putting up a bit of a fight when Susan and her daughter tried to lead him into the trailer."

Krista's hands flew up to her mouth.

Summer Shadows

"Whose trailer?"

The old man shook his head. "I don't know. It was a battered old thing. I've never seen it before. But, as I said, I did hear Susan shouting at the pony and there was a lot of kicking and neighing before they finally got him inside. I remember them talking to the man with the trailer and I believe money changed hands before he drove the pony away."

"Drove him away!" Krista echoed faintly. She pictured Drifter being dragged down the overgrown path and shoved into the unknown trailer. "Do you know where the driver took him?" she asked desperately.

The old man shook his head with an air of finality. "I have absolutely no idea."

Chapter Eight

Shining Star lowered his head to listen to Krista's explanation. "If we are too late to rescue Drifter, I must return to Galishe, at least for a day."

Krista's hopes sank. The sun beat down strongly as her magical pony rose from the ground. "Must you leave?" she asked.

The wise pony nodded. "I have other tasks in other worlds. But I will come back soon."

"But Drifter needs you here," Krista reminded him.

"Even I cannot be in two places at once,"

Star said gently. "My brother, North Star, is calling me home to Galishe."

Puzzled, Krista noticed for the first time a fast moving cloud draw near and descend around them, shedding a glittering light. "There are others like you?" she asked eagerly. "More magical ponies?"

Shining Star nodded. "There is Pale Moon, my sister, and Great Bear, our father. Look – North Star has come to fetch me."

And sure enough, a second beautiful pony appeared in the mist. If possible, his coat shone more brightly than Shining Star's and his wings were wider. He carried his head more proudly and his mane was softer and more silken than anything Krista had ever seen.

She gasped at the wonderful sight. "Come, my brother!" The new pony spoke to Star in the same wise manner. "Our father has a task for us in a land far from here. We must complete it before nightfall."

"Remember Drifter!" Krista called as the two ponies rose higher.

"I will return tomorrow, at sunrise," Shining Star promised.

"And while you're away, I will try and find out exactly what Susan Owen has done with Drifter!" Krista decided, gritting her teeth.

The magical ponies' beating wings created a welcome breeze.

"Good. Will you call at Lane End?" Star asked before he departed.

One surprise meeting with the hard-faced woman was enough, so she shook her head. "I can't do that," she explained, as he flew higher. "But I think I know someone who can!"

"This is the plan!" Krista told Janey Bellwood. She'd made her way on foot back to Hartfell and found Janey in the stable yard, tacking up Misty and looking forward to a trek. In a rush of words Krista had explained what had happened to poor Drifter.

Janey had looked upset and said she would do anything she could to help.

"We'll ask Jo if we can ride out by ourselves," Krista gabbled. "I'll saddle Comanche and we'll ride over to Oxtoby. Then you knock at Susan Owen's door!"

"I do?" Janey asked in a puzzled tone.

"Yes. She already met me and turfed me off her land. So I hide while you pretend that you want to buy Drifter from her – you've seen him in the field and it doesn't look like anyone is riding him, so you thought they might want to sell him, blah-blah!"

"OK!" Janey agreed, quickly understanding Krista's plan. "Then she tells me he's already been sold, and I ask her who to and she gives me the name and address of this man with the trailer!"

"You've got it!" Krista cried. Janey was cool for agreeing to help. If they could get this far, then their problem was practically solved!

"Let's go!" Janey said, springing into the saddle and turning Misty towards the gate.

"OK, go and knock!" Krista urged, holding Comanche back while Janey dismounted from Misty and stood at the gate of Susan Owen's house.

They'd got there in record time, trotting all the way. Both ponies were breathing hard. "Stand, Misty!" Krista ordered, dismounting from Comanche and ducking down behind the hedge while Janey went up the garden path.

Janey knocked and waited.

"I hope this works!" Krista whispered to Comanche. Time was slipping by.

Already Drifter might be far away.

"Hi!" they heard Janey say to whoever answered the door. "Is your mum in?"

"Maybe," came the suspicious reply. "Why do you want her?"

"I wanted to ask about the pony in the field," Janey went on boldly. "I saw him the other day and wondered if you wanted to sell him."

"Good for her!" Krista breathed. She risked peering over the hedge to see a short, wavy-haired girl of about nine frowning at Janey, about to close the front door in her face.

"Too late!" the girl snapped. "He's gone!"

"Wait!" Janey cried. "What d'you mean, he's gone?"

"We sold him. Bye!"

The door slammed and Krista's heart sank. But Janey didn't give in. She knocked again at the door.

This time it was Susan Owen who answered. "Didn't you hear what Maisie said?" she demanded. "The pony was completely useless. He wouldn't do a single thing he was told, so we sold him!"

Krista cowered behind the hedge and held her breath.

Janey kept her nerve. "Would you tell me who to?" she asked politely.

"What for? No one in their right mind would want the useless creature!" Like her daughter, Susan Owen wanted to get rid of Janey as fast as possible. "The only person who might possibly have a use for him was another dealer, so that's who I sold him to."

"Where does he or she live?" Janey asked.

"He," Mrs Owen grunted.

"What's his name?"

Drifter's ex-owner tutted impatiently. "Maisie!" she yelled. "What was that horse dealer's name?"

"Somebody Turnbull!" came the reply.

"That's it!" her mother remembered, ready to slam the door again. "His name's Bill Turnbull, but he's not from Oxtoby. He's from Maythorne. *Now* are you satisfied?"

Chapter Nine

That afternoon, at the stables, Krista helped Jo with chores around the yard, all the time remembering the wonderful sight of the two magical ponies flying out to sea. She tried not to think too much about Drifter.

"Hey Krista, what happened to you earlier this morning?" Jo asked, lifting a straw bale from the wheelbarrow and taking it into Apollo's stable.

"I had something to do before I came here," Krista said quickly, picking Lucy up from the floor and carrying her out of

Jo's way. The black cat purred and licked Krista's hand.

"There's nothing wrong, is there?" Jo asked, cutting the twine that held the bale together and asking Krista to help her make a clean bed for her thoroughbred.

"No," she fibbed, then dashed on with the question she'd been longing to ask. "But I was wondering – do you know a man called Bill Turnbull?"

Jo took a rest from spreading straw. "He's a horse dealer, isn't he?"

Krista nodded, expecting more.

"But not one that I'd recommend," Jo said with a frown. "He has a bad name in the horse world."

My Magical Pony

Krista swallowed hard. This was what she'd been afraid of! "How come?" she asked, seizing a hayfork to spread the straw more evenly.

"He doesn't treat his animals well. They're usually pretty thin and neglected by the time he takes them to auction."

"And then what happens?"

Jo looked sharply at Krista. "Are you sure you want to know? It's not a very pleasant story."

Krista gulped and nodded. "Go ahead."

"Well, Turnbull's animals are so worn out and poor-looking that they're usually sold on to an even more dubious owner, who probably intends to have them put down, and turned into pet food ..."

Summer Shadows

"Don't!" Krista exclaimed. This was even worse than she'd expected.

"I did warn you," Jo reminded her. "I'm sorry, Krista, but it's not a very nice world sometimes."

Awful! Horrible! Krista couldn't bear to think about the traders' cruelty. It mustn't happen to Drifter! It couldn't!

The shadow hanging over Drifter was now so dark that Krista couldn't pretend to be cheerful.

Janey noticed how sad she was and took her to one side.

"Has something bad happened since this morning?" she asked, sitting with Krista on the bench outside the tack room.

"No, but I have to rescue Drifter even more than before!" she confided. "Janey, I can't let him stay with Bill Turnbull!"

Janey stared at the dusty ground. "Even if you find this Maythorne place, I don't see how you can get Drifter away – unless you pay the man a lot of money."

"Which I haven't got!" Krista moaned.

"Or steal him," Janey said, as a casual, throwaway line. But then she saw the stubborn light in Krista's eyes and hurried on with a warning. "Which means you'd be in dead trouble! And anyway, it would be too difficult."

Still Krista had that stubborn look.

"Then, if you did manage to steal him, what would you do with him?" Janey tried to get through to Krista, who by now was biting her lip and frowning. "You couldn't bring him back here to Hartfell because Jo would never agree to it. Are you listening, Krista? What good can you do?"

Janey's common sense got through to Krista at last and upset her. She stood up and began to walk away. "If I don't do anything, Drifter is going to die!"

Janey ran after her. "Stop! Listen! It's too dangerous!"

But Krista wouldn't turn back. She was going to save Drifter's life, whatever it took. And she was going to do it with Shining Star!

It was high summer and birdsong broke the night silence before four o'clock in the morning.

Krista had counted every minute of darkness, not sleeping a wink but sitting by the window, staring out at the stars. Her bed lay undisturbed.

Shining Star had promised her that he would return at sunrise, and so, as the birds began to sing and a grey light crept into the sky, she sat scarcely breathing, hoping every second that her magical pony would appear.

Summer Shadows

She heard the tick of the clock in the hallway, the rustle of small animals in the hedge below her window.

"Come back!" she whispered, straining her eyes to make out shapes in the dim light.

Then a glow of pink tinged the grey, and a hint of gold. The sun was rising at last!

My Magical Pony

With the sun came Shining Star. He flew over the eastern hilltop, surrounded by a silver glow, beating his great wings. A cloud of glittering dust fell from his back to the dewy ground.

He saw Krista's pale, sleepless face and spoke kindly. "I told you I would return," he murmured. "I have completed my task with North Star. Now it is time for us to save your injured friend."

Chapter Ten

"What are you most afraid of?" Star asked Krista as they rose into the sky.

They soared over the moors, cresting hills and swooping down into valleys until they reached the coast.

"That we're too late," she confessed. Almost a whole day had gone by since Bill Turnbull had driven off with Drifter.

As they flew, the magical pony gazed ahead. "I see a dark place full of shadows," he said softly. "A creature is hurt and crying out. But he is still alive!"

My Magical Pony

"Thank heavens!" Krista whispered. She reminded herself that Star had the gift of seeing and hearing things that were impossible for ordinary beings, so she trusted this vision. And she knew that they would soon arrive in Maythorne.

Shining Star beat his wings and they flew swiftly over Whitton Bay, beyond Black Point, following the shore. They passed over small seaside towns, still asleep at this time on a Sunday morning, until they came to the village where the horse dealer lived.

Krista's heart beat faster as the magical pony landed on the empty beach.

"I hear the cry of the little pony," Star said, turning his head inland and setting out

towards some sand dunes. He strode swiftly.
Krista looked ahead anxiously, holding tight
as they passed through the hilly dunes and
came into the small town.

Star trotted towards a crossroads and
listened intently. He was silent as he chose

the road out of town, across a level stretch of rough grassland.

"Soon!" Krista promised Drifter, her whole body and mind concentrating on the rescue.

At the first turning in the road, the magical pony hesitated. "All is quiet," he told Krista.

"So which way do we go?" Glancing to their left, down a narrow lane, she spotted deep ruts in the bare earth – a sign that a heavy vehicle often passed that way. "Let's try this," she decided.

Star trotted swiftly between the high hedges until they came to a field with many horses.

"Wait!" Krista whispered. She took in the scene – there were broken fences patched with barbed wire, and the horses and ponies looked thin and miserable. Beyond the field was a small, shabby house with old outbuildings. "This must be the place!"

Star went forward slowly. "Your pony is not far from here," he predicted, heading straight for the broken-down buildings at the end of the lane. "We must be quiet now, and creep in unnoticed!"

Thinking it best to go forward on foot, Krista slipped from the magical pony on to the ground. They entered a yard and saw an old wheelbarrow propped against a wall, empty plastic feed sacks piled in a corner, and a tell-tale old trailer parked in front of the cottage. As she stopped to take in her surroundings,

Star didn't hesitate, but walked straight to the door of the nearest outbuilding.

"Come!" he told Krista.

With dread in her heart, she went and eased open the rickety door.

Inside there were broken bales of straw, dirty buckets and rusty parts of an old tractor.

Summer Shadows

It was dark and smelly, there were cobwebs, old rags, tins of paint and boxes of nails jumbled everywhere. And although she couldn't see at first, Krista knew there was an animal here in this dark, unpleasant place.

A creature was breathing; his presence filled the air.

"Drifter?" Krista murmured.

There was a low whinny of distress, a cry for help.

And as her eyes adjusted to the dark, Krista saw the chestnut pony, wearing a head collar and tethered in a far corner, paralysed by fear. He stood with his head hanging, knees bleeding, his whole body trembling.

She ran to him, intending to untie the rope,

but the frightened pony backed off and
tugged wildly, trying to rear up and strike out
with his hoofs.

"Drifter, it's me!" she cried. "I'm your
friend!"

The pony snorted and breathed heavily,
his eyes rolled with fear.

Shining Star came forward to calm Drifter,
walking up to him and putting his head close,
breathing comfort over him, until Krista was
at last able to move in and untie the rope.

"Good boy!" she soothed, knowing that
they had to get Drifter out of here.

In the small, cramped space, Shining Star
had to back out towards the door, followed
by Krista and a still-trembling Drifter.

Summer Shadows

Then they were all out in the yard, breathing in the fresh air.

"He is very weak," Star told Krista, warning her not to hurry the injured pony, whose steps were slow and shaky.

But she knew they had to make a quick getaway. "Come on, boy!" she urged, trying to lead him across the yard.

Just then the cottage door flew open and a man dressed in T-shirt and jeans ran out. He carried a long horse whip which he snaked towards them to cut across their path. "Stop right where you are!" he yelled.

Shocked, Krista did as she was told. She felt Drifter pull back. At her side, Star stood his ground, though the tip of the whip flicked close to his nose.

"Put that pony back where you found him!"
the angry Bill Turnbull ordered. He was a
small man, but thick-set, with a shaved head.
Obviously he had got out of bed in a hurry
because his feet were bare.

Poor Drifter was still pulling away from
Krista, neighing shrilly. She held tight to his
lead rope. "How could you be so cruel?"
she cried. "His knees are bleeding, he can
hardly walk!"

"Well, he's fit for nothing anyway. It's a
waste of time giving him first aid before I get
rid of him!" Turnbull replied, trying to drive
Shining Star back with his whip. He flicked it
again, and this time the tip struck home.

Summer Shadows

Star reared
up, threatening
to trample his
attacker.

Anger flamed inside
Krista. "Put that whip
down!" she yelled.

"No way! You drop that
lead rope and leave while you still can!"
Turnbull advanced another step or two, but
halted when Star once more reared up.

"Yes, let go of the rope," Star told Krista.
"I'll look after the pony if you find some way
to distract the man."

She had to think fast, remembering the
junk in the outbuilding, wondering if there

was anything there that might help. "Go with Star!" she whispered to Drifter then quickly ran back in.

Turnbull meanwhile raised his cruel whip against the grey moorland pony, yelling at him to get back. Instead, Star lowered his head and charged at the horse dealer, swerving at the last second and herding Drifter towards the gate.

Krista came back out into the yard to see the man stagger backwards and then regain his balance. She was carrying a box full of rusty nails which she tipped and flung towards him. The nails scattered far and wide. "Try treading on those in bare feet!" she yelled.

Turnbull cried out in pain as he trod on the

nails. Suddenly he was trapped, unable to move anywhere except back into his house.

"Good!" Star told Krista. "This gives us time." He turned to Drifter, who stayed close at his side, trembling in case the man came after them. "Now, my friend, you must walk even though it is painful for you!"

Krista saw how difficult it was for the chestnut. His eyes were dull, his legs stiff. "Walk!" she urged, knowing that it was only a matter of time before Bill Turnbull put on his shoes and came after them. "Trot if you can!"

Drifter made a big effort to keep up with Star, who led the way down the lane. Behind them, they heard a door slam, then the start of an engine.

"He's coming after us in his car!" Krista gasped. "What do we do now?"

Shining Star thought quickly. "Open the field gate!" he told her. "We will hide behind the hedge."

Krista glanced over the gate at Turnbull's other startled horses. With fumbling fingers, she pressed the latch and opened it. Within seconds, she, Drifter and Star were out of sight – just in time, because Turnbull's Land Rover quickly appeared, engine roaring, rattling past them without stopping.

"Thank heavens!" Krista breathed.

"Now we will cut across the field and go through the gate," Star decided. "After that we can walk across country, back to the beach."

Summer Shadows

So they crossed the field, ignoring the curious approach of the horses, quietly slipping away from the cold-hearted dealer before he discovered his mistake.

Once on the open hillside, Krista, Drifter and Shining Star paused for breath.

"We did it!" Krista sighed.

"Yes, you did well," Star agreed. But he turned to look at Drifter. "Can you carry on?" he asked.

Drifter put one foot forward and then another, but he was in pain. And still he trembled from head to foot.

"I think he has a fever," Star told Krista. "He has courage, but no strength."

Krista thought of the long trek ahead.
"Come on, Drifter, you must try!"

The grateful pony took another few steps
before Krista decided she would try to cover
his bleeding knees. Stooping down, she took
off her over-shirt and tore down the seams
to make rough bandages that she gently
wrapped around each front leg. "When we
reach the sea, I can cool you down with sea
water," she promised.

Drifter looked pleadingly at Star.

"Try!" the magical pony said.

"You can make it!" Krista insisted.

So gamely and wincing at every step, the
neglected pony made his slow way down to
the sea.

Chapter Eleven

With every step he took towards the beach Drifter grew weaker.

"He's sweating badly!" Krista murmured to Shining Star. "It must be a fever – either from eating the ragwort, or from the infected cuts!"

"You have your freedom!" Star told the little chestnut. "Do not give in now!"

Gathering his courage, Drifter stumbled on through the heather.

It's so sad! Krista thought. She had a memory of Drifter in his field at Hartfell – his coat shining like a new conker fresh from its green shell, with his dazzling white star and his long, silky mane. How he used to trot and prance, dancing across the meadow towards her! And she looked at him now – caked in mud, limping and sweating. "I'm scared!" she whispered to Shining Star, fearing that every step could be Drifter's last.

"You are through the worst," Star told the suffering pony. "We will reach the shore and you can rest."

The magical pony's soothing words seemed to drag Drifter forward until at last the sea shore at Maythorne came into view.

"You see!" Krista cried, patting his neck softly. "You're a brave boy! You're doing amazingly well!"

Summer Shadows

Drifter staggered on through the sand dunes, but when he came to the wet sand, his strength gave out and he sank on to his side.

"Oh no!" Krista knew that the pony must not lie for long. She held up his head and gave him more words of encouragement.

In the background, white waves broke and crashed on to the beach, sending cool white wavelets running up the beach towards the dunes.

"His will to live is ebbing," Star said in a solemn voice.

"Get up, Drifter!" Krista pleaded. He looked worse than ever, now that the sand had stuck to his wet coat. "I know your legs hurt, but you must stand!"

My Magical Pony

Shining Star came close and lowered his head to speak to Drifter. "Have courage!" he urged.

Drifter took a deep breath then with a whinny of pain he struggled back on to his feet, prepared to follow his rescuers until his final breath.

Slowly, step by step, Krista and Star led him to the shelter of a high dune.

"He must rest," Star told her. "We will leave him and fly to fetch fresh water and perhaps food. At least the trader will not find him now."

"How can we leave him?" Krisa cried. She helped to ease the pony on to his side once more. He lay helpless in the pale sand, gasping for breath.

"We must." The magical pony's decision was firm. "He needs water if he is to live!"

Krista fell to her knees and whispered to Drifter. "We won't be long!" she promised. "We'll be back as soon as we can!"

Drifter tried to raise his head, but it sank back on to the sand.

"Come!" Star said. So she climbed on his back, and with a strong beat of his wings, they were in the air.

My Magical Pony

Shining Star's flight was swift. "Where will we find water and food for your friend?" he asked Krista.

"At Hartfell!" she decided, her heart beating fast as she looked down on the villages and the moorland below. They could be there in minutes, and she would be sure to find what they needed at Jo's stables. Shining Star could wait in the lane while she dashed into the yard.

So the magical pony flew faster than they had ever flown, his mane flowing back from his neck, his tail streaming behind him. The wind whipped Krista's breath away, so that she had to lean forward and put her head against Star's shimmering neck for shelter.

Summer Shadows

Soon he landed in the lane outside the stable yard. "Make haste!" he said.

Krista slid from his back and ran into the yard. She saw that it was still too early for the Sunday morning trek. The yard was quiet. There was no sign of Jo.

But as Krista ran towards the tack room to grab a water container, a stable door opened and the owner emerged.

"Hi, Krista!"

Jo's cheerful call stopped her in her tracks. Krista was breathing heavily, thinking fast. "Hi. Listen, Jo – I've just seen Drifter!"

Jo cocked her head to one side. "How come?"

"I was out on the beach – you know Star,

that grey moorland pony I sometimes ride bareback? Well, we were messing about in Maythorne Bay, and I don't know how it happened, but we found Drifter wandering all alone in the dunes. He's sick, Jo!"

The stable owner put down the hayfork she was carrying and came across the yard. "How sick?" she asked in a worried voice.

"Really sick!" Krista gasped. "He's lame and he's got a

fever. I'm going to ride straight back with some water and food. Can you bring medicine for the fever?"

"Antibiotics?" Jo quizzed. "Is it that serious?"

Krista nodded. "He's going to die if we don't help him!" Grabbing the container, she ran it under the yard tap, splashing her legs and feet in her hurry. "Drifter's in the dunes at the edge of Maythorne beach. Come with the medicine!" she urged.

Without giving Jo time to think or argue, Krista lifted the lid of a food barrel and scooped some into a plastic bag which she shoved into her jacket pocket. Then, picking up the water container, she dashed out of the yard.

My Magical Pony

Seconds later, she was climbing up on to Star's back and they were on their way once more.

Maythorne beach was still deserted when Shining Star and Krista returned. The waves crashed against the shore, the early sun cast long shadows amongst the dunes.

Their earlier footprints showed them where to find the sick pony, so Star landed close by and Krista ran the last few metres into the dunes.

"Drifter!" she called.

She saw him lying still and for a moment she thought they were too late.

"Drifter, open your eyes, look up!" she

pleaded, falling to her knees and quickly unscrewing the water container.

The sound of her voice drifted into his consciousness. Slowly he opened his eyes. His breathing was shallow, but he was still alive.

Krista offered him cool water from the palm of her hand and let it dribble into the side of his mouth. "Drink this!"

The pony swallowed. He raised his head for more.

"Let him drink, then we must ask him to stand," Shining Star said.

Krista nodded. She offered more water, then unwound the strips of cloth from his knees and cooled his wounds with more liquid.

They were encrusted with dirt and ugly, but not deep. "You heard what Star said!" she whispered, taking hold of Drifter's shabby head collar, ready to help him. "You have to try to stand up!"

He understood and he was brave, struggling to bend his front legs and make them take his weight. It took a long time and it hurt him a lot, but at last he did it.

"Good boy!" Krista felt tears spring to her eyes, but she knew they were tears of relief. Drifter looked a sorry sight – covered in sand and mud, still trembling and bleeding – but the water had done the trick. He was standing, he was fighting to live!

Summer Shadows

"Give him food," Shining Star said quietly, looking at Krista's tears and wondering about them.

Drifter's head was lowered and he was eating out of Krista's cupped hand when Jo's Land Rover and trailer rattled on to the beach.

Jo saw Krista from a distance and ran to join her. She had someone with her, and when Krista looked up she saw it was Janey Bellwood.

"Poor Drifter!" Janey cried.

Quickly Jo took a syringe from a medicine pack which she carried. She took a look at his dull eyes and sweating skin then injected an antibiotic into the pony's shoulder. "How did he get into this state?" she asked with a frown and a shake of her head.

"It's a long story!" Krista sighed. Thank goodness Jo had arrived. Now they could get Drifter away from Maythorne beach and back to safety.

A few metres away, Shining Star looked on quietly.

"Mum and Dad dropped me off in the yard and Jo told us what had happened to Drifter!" Janey explained to Krista once they had brought the chestnut pony back to Hartfell.

Krista had driven in the Land Rover with the others, leaving Star on Maythorne beach.

"Look for me later in the day," Star had whispered to Krista as he watched them leave.

"I told Dad I wanted to come and help!" Janey insisted. She was sitting beside Krista on a bale of straw in Drifter's old stable. The chestnut's knees were freshly bandaged, his coat was brushed free of sand and mud. Jo had said that the medicine would soon work and Drifter's fever would fade away. Meanwhile, she'd asked an officer from the RSPCA to go and investigate the plight of the poor horses at Bill Turnbull's place.

My Magical Pony

Krista nodded. "We were just in time!" she sighed.

"You saved Drifter's life!" Janey said, her eyes shining with tears.

Me and my magical pony! Krista thought with a smile. Once she was sure that brave Drifter was on the road to recovery, she would return to the magic spot once again.

"Jo still says Drifter isn't a riding school pony," Janey went on. She leaned back against the wall, looking up at the stable ceiling. "I tried to talk her into having him back for good, but she said he was a pony that needed a good rider, not learners."

Krista stood up and went to stroke Drifter's neck. *What now?* she wondered. Sure, she and

Star had saved the pony's life, but what would happen to him next?

There was a silence until Janey took up from where she'd left off. "I just explained the problem to Dad – that Drifter's new owners had done this to him. Dad thinks it's awful too!"

"It is!" Krista agreed. The excitement in Janey's voice made her wonder. "And?" she urged.

Janey's bright eyes stared back at Krista. "Dad and Mum had a talk."

"And?" Krista said again.

"Mum wasn't very happy at first ..."

"But?"

"But in the end she agreed!" Janey's face broke into a big grin.

Krista's mouth fell open. "To do what?" she cried.

"To *buy* Drifter!" Janey exclaimed. "To buy him and keep him here at Hartfell, so I can ride him any time I want!"

Summary Shadows

*

Krista had left Janey in Drifter's stable and run all the way to the magic spot. The sun was high in the sky, there were no shadows on the cliff path – only white butterflies settling on the flowers and the stillness of a calm summer's day.

Shining Star was waiting for her return, wings outstretched. "You are happy!" he said, tossing his head.

"We got Drifter safely home!" she cried.

"Home?" he asked.

"To Hartfell. It's where he's going to live from now on!" And she told the magical pony about Janey Bellwood.

"A kind owner." Star gave a satisfied nod.

My Magical Pony

Krista felt the breeze from his wings. "Thank you!" she said, over and over. There had been times when she'd thought Drifter wouldn't make it, even with Star's magic on their side.

"The kind hearts have overcome the cruel ones," Star pointed out. He beat his wings and rose from the ground.

"Will you come back again?" Krista asked, tilting her head to follow his flight.

"When I am needed," he promised. He flew higher into the blue sky, heading out to sea. "Goodbye, Krista my friend, until next time."

"Goodbye!" she called.